RITA THE RESCUER

Rita on the River

Also by Hilda Offen:
Rita Rides Again

RITA THE RESCUER

Rita on the River

Hilda Offen

troika books

For Michael Andrew Caulfield

Published by TROIKA BOOKS

First published 2016

1 3 5 7 9 10 8 6 4 2

Text and illustrations copyright © Hilda Offen 2016

The moral rights of the author/illustrator have been asserted

A CIP catalogue record for this book is available from the British Library

ISBN   978-1-909991-21-7

Printed in Poland

Troika Books
Well House, Green Lane, Ardleigh CO7 7PD, UK

www.troikabooks.com

"At last! Here we are at the river!" said
Grandad Potter.

"Hooray!" said Eddie. "Jim and I are going
on a canoe."

"And I'll take Julie and Rita out on a punt,"
said Grandad Potter. "I'm an expert at this,
girls – you'll see."

"First of all, we'd better hire some life jackets," said Grandad Potter.

"I'm sorry," said the man in the boat-house. "I've only got four left – and they're all in bigger sizes."

"Never mind, Rita," said Grandad Potter. "You can sit on the bank and watch the ducks. We won't be long."

"You can get the picnic ready," said Julie
and the other two giggled.

Rita waited till the others had disappeared round a bend in the river. Then she ducked behind a willow.

"It's a good thing I brought my outfit!" she thought.

The next moment she stepped out into the open – and there stood Rita the Rescuer!

Not a moment too soon! A scream rang out. A puppy had fallen off a bridge into the river. It was struggling to stay afloat. Rita zoomed through the air and – Splash! She dived into the water and grabbed the puppy. Then she swam with it to the bank. The owner came puffing up to join them.

My little Bertie! However can I thank you, Rescuer?

But Rita was hurtling off again. She'd heard another scream.

9

Timmy Parker was being chased by a
swan. He'd been throwing sticks at its nest
and it was very angry.

Rita snatched Timmy and shot into the
sky. The swan flew after them. But Rita
moved so fast that after a while it gave up
and went back to its nest.

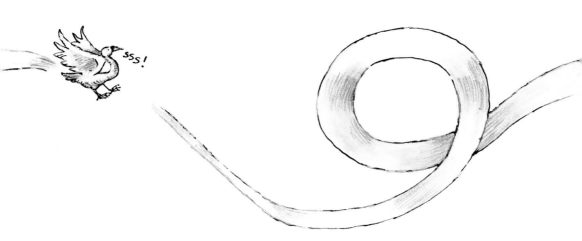

"I shouldn't throw sticks again if I were you," said Rita, landing Timmy next to his parents. "Sorry – I've got to go!"

She could hear Julie screaming "Grandad! My Grandad!"

Grandad Potter's punting pole had stuck fast in the mud.

"Help!" screamed Julie as the punt drifted on without him.

Rita was there in the twinkling of an eye. She grabbed Grandad Potter's life-jacket and tugged. "Slurp!" went the pole as it squelched out of the mud.

"I don't suppose there's any chance of an
autograph, Rescuer?" Julie called as she and
Grandad Potter floated on their way. Rita
had no time to answer; her sharp eyes had
spotted something unusual.

A bottle was drifting past in the current.
And Rita could see that there was
something inside.

HELP!
I'm starving!
I'm stranded
on an
island.

She dived in and grabbed the bottle. Out fell a letter. She straightened it out and read it.

"I must find the island!" thought Rita. "There's no time to lose."

Rita flew high into the sky and in the distance she spotted a small island. She could see someone waving at the edge of the trees – someone in ragged trousers who was looking very thin and weak.

"Hooray!" he gasped. "Am I pleased to see you, Rescuer! I've been here for days. My boat sank and I just managed to struggle to this island. I'm starving!"

"Why didn't you call for help?" asked Rita.

"I did," whispered the man. "But I caught a cold and I've lost my voice. I tried waving, but people just waved back at me. And I can't swim."

"Come on then," said Rita and she flew him back to the river bank. They shook hands and the man tottered off to find a café.

"My Trevor dived in!" sobbed Mrs Pike.
"And he hasn't come up again."

"Leave it to me!" said Rita.

Trevor was at the bottom of the river,
all tangled up in a supermarket trolley.

18

Uh-oh! Got to go—
Eddie and Jim need m

Rita freed his leg and carried him to
the bank.

She brought the trolley back, too,
so no-one else would get caught.

19

Oh no! Her brothers were in big trouble.
They'd gone too far down river and
their canoe was about to be swept over
a waterfall.

"Help!" screamed Eddie and Jim.

DANGER

"Here I come!" called Rita.
She caught the canoe in mid-air and
carried it back up river to a safer place.

Thank you, thank you, Rescuer!" gasped Eddie and Jim; but Rita couldn't stay to talk – there was more work for her to do.

A giant crocodile was about to attack some swimmers. It opened its terrible jaws and –

"Not so fast!" cried Rita.

Rita leaped into the river and wrestled
with the crocodile. Over and over they
went. Rita clung on tight and wouldn't
let go. She clamped the crocodile's jaws
together and at last it stopped struggling.

"If I take my hands away, will you promise to stop attacking people?" said Rita.

The crocodile nodded, so Rita released it. Then it started crying great big crocodile tears.

"I've escaped from the zoo!" it said. "I didn't like it there. Boo-hoo! I wish I was back in Africa."

"Hold on tight, then!" said Rita. "If we hurry, I can still be back in time for tea."

Rita hoisted the crocodile onto her back. Then, moving at supersonic speed, they shot into the sky.

When they reached the River Nile, Rita landed the crocodile on a sandbank, alongside its old friends. Then she was off again.

She got back to the river in double-quick time. She even had time to win a rowing race.

After that she darted behind the willow tree and changed back into little Rita Potter.

By the time the others returned, she had the picnic all ready for them.

"You missed the Rescuer again, Rita!" said Julie. "She saved Grandad."

"And she stopped me and Jim from being swept over a waterfall!" cried Eddie.

"How were the ducks, Rita?" asked Grandad Potter.

"Very interesting," said Rita. She could see Julie staring at her medal. "Oh look! Is that a water vole over there?'"

Look out for another Rita title from Troika Books

RITA RIDES AGAIN

*Rita is the youngest of the Potter family.
Sometimes it seems as if she's missing out on all the
excitement. But Rita has an amazing double life, appearing
as Rita the Rescuer whenever there's a challenge to be
faced. "Thank you Rescuer, that was a close one!"
Whether it's ghosts in the castle, monsters in the moat or
a flock of angry peacocks, you can count on the Rescuer!*